First published in the United States, Great Britain, Canada, Australia, and New Zealand in 2010
by North-South Books Inc., an imprint of NordSüd Verlag AG, CH-8005 Zürich, Switzerland.
Distributed in the United States by North-South Books Inc., New York 10001.

Library of Congress Cataloging-in-Publication Data is available.
ISBN: 978-0-7358-2280-1 (trade edition)
1 3 5 7 9 • 10 8 6 4 2
Printed in Belgium by Proost N.V., B 2300 Turnhout, November 2009.
www.northsouth.com

FSC
Mixed Sources
Product group from well-managed
forests and other controlled sources

Cert no. BV-COC-070303
www.fsc.org
© 1996 Forest Stewardship Council

Marcus Pfister

Happy Birthday, Bertie!

NorthSouth
New York / London

Today is Bertie's birthday.

"Happy Birthday, Bertie," says Daddy and gives him a big birthday kiss.

Bertie's friends are coming soon. He wants to be nice and clean for his birthday party, so he takes a bath. Bertie could sit in the tub for hours. He loves splashing in the water. He's hoping that Daddy will give him water goggles for his birthday.

"Hurry up, Bertie," calls Daddy. "We still have lots to do."

"First I want to open my present!" says Bertie.

"One thing at a time, Birthday Boy," says Daddy. "First we have to bake a cake."

Bertie helps by stirring the batter and licking the spoon. Then Daddy and Bertie cover the whole cake with a thick layer of chocolate frosting. They decorate it with candies and candles.

"Can I have my present now?" asks Bertie.

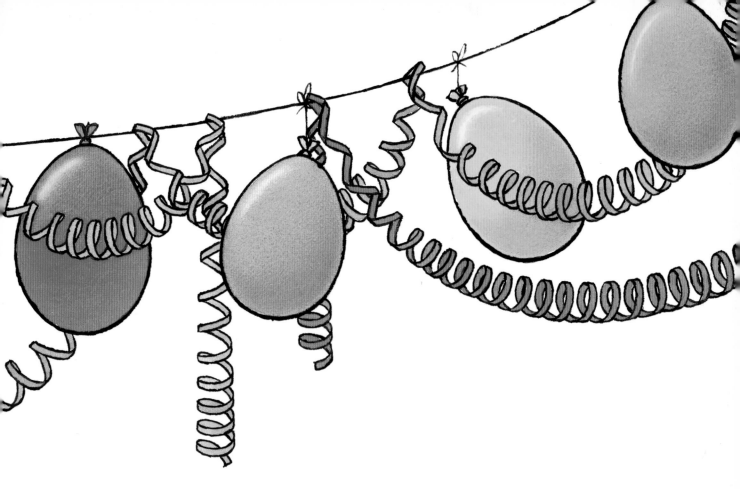

"Not until we've put up the decorations," says Daddy.
"Every birthday party needs decorations."

So they hang streamers, and blow up brightly colored balloons, and hang those up too.

"Careful, Bertie," says Daddy. "Don't fall off that chair."

"Now can I unwrap my present?" Bertie asks.

But just at that moment, the doorbell rings.

Bertie runs to the door and throws it open. There are Alex and Hannah and Benny. They stare at all the decorations.

"Come in!" says Daddy. "The party's in here."

"Come in!" says Bertie.

Bertie's friends have all brought presents. Bertie stacks
them on the table in the hallway.

Daddy would like to put his present there too, but he has
forgotten where it is. He didn't want Bertie to find it, so he
hid it. Now *he* can't find it.

"Before we eat cake and unwrap presents, how about a game?" says Daddy. "You all hide, and Bertie will try to find you." Daddy will try to find his present.

Bertie finds Hannah first, hiding under the kitchen table giggling.

Something smells good. What can it be? The cake of course! Hannah's and Bertie's mouths start to water.

"No one will know if we take just a little piece," says Bertie.

Bertie finds Alex next, hiding behind the coats in the hallway. But there's something even more interesting in the hallway. Presents!

"No one will know if we take just a little peek," says Bertie. "What do you think, Alex?"

Now there is only Benny to find. Where could he be?

Benny is trying to make himself look small on top of the cupboard.

"I can see you!" yells Bertie.

Bertie's shout makes Benny jump. Down he tumbles, pulling all the decorations with him.

Daddy comes running in. "Is everything ok? Did you hurt yourselves?"

Bertie and Benny are sitting on the floor in a jumble of streamers and balloons. But what is that in the middle of the muddle? A bright blue package. It's Daddy's present for Bertie! He had hidden it on top of the cupboard!

Daddy is so happy to find it. He tells them the story of the lost present, and everyone laughs.

Soon the mess is cleaned up and the four friends sit down at the table. Daddy lights the candles and brings in the cake. They all sing "Happy Birthday." Bertie makes a wish and blows out the candles.

Finally it's time for Bertie to open his presents. He already knows what's inside two of the boxes: a red ball from Hannah and a great book from Benny. He opens Alex's present. It's a rubber ring for swimming!

But what did Daddy get him? Bertie can't wait to find out. Is it . . . ?

It is! It's diving goggles! They will go perfectly with the rubber swimming ring.

"Can we go to the pool tomorrow?" Bertie begs. "I'm going to learn how to swim!"

It feels like it just began, but suddenly the party is over and Bertie's friends have to go home.

Bertie gives Hannah, Alex, and Benny a big hug. "You are my three best friends in the whole world," he tells them.

At bedtime, Bertie gives Daddy a big hug too. "Thank you, Daddy," he says. "This was my best birthday ever!"